Working for our Future

Ending Poverty and Hunger

Judith Anderson with Christian Aid

SEA-TO-SEA

Mankato Collingwood London

This edition first published in 2010 by
Sea-to-Sea Publications
Distributed by Black Rabbit Books
P.O. Box 3263, Mankato, Minnesota 56002

Printed in USA

Library of Congress Cataloging-in-Publication Data

Anderson, Judith (Judith Mary)
  Ending poverty and hunger / Judith Anderson with Christian Aid.
     p. cm. -- (Working for our future)
  Includes index.
  ISBN 978-1-59771-195-1 (hardcover)
 1. Poverty. 2. Poor. 3. Poor families. 4. Economic history. I. Christian Aid. II. Title.
  HC79.P63A63 2010
  363.8--dc22
                          2008044881

9 8 7 6 5 4 3 2

Published by arrangement with the Watts Publishing Group Ltd., London.

Editor: Jeremy Smith
Art director: Jonathan Hair
Design: Rita Storey

Produced in association with Christian Aid. Franklin Watts would like to thank Christian Aid for their help with this title, in particular for allowing permission to use the information concerning Chus Echevarría, Binta Tapile, and Servina Marta which is © Christian Aid. We would also like to thank the parents of Shauna Adams for the information and photographs provided.

Picture credits: Adrian Arbib/Christian Aid: 3br, 10l, 13t, 16b, 24b. Alamy: 1, 4b, 6t, 10t, 11b, 13b, 25. Annabel Davis/Christian Aid: 3bc, 6b, 7, 12t, 20-21 all. Eduardo Martino/Christian Aid: 3bl, 8-9 all, 15b, 19b, 23t. istockphoto.com: 27b.

The Millennium Development Goals

In 2000, government leaders agreed on eight goals to help build a better, fairer world in the 21st century. These goals include getting rid of extreme poverty, fighting child mortality and disease, promoting education, gender equality, and maternal health, and ensuring sustainable development.

The aim of this series is to look at the problems these goals address, show how they are being tackled at local level, and relate them to the experiences of children around the world.

Contents

The Cast

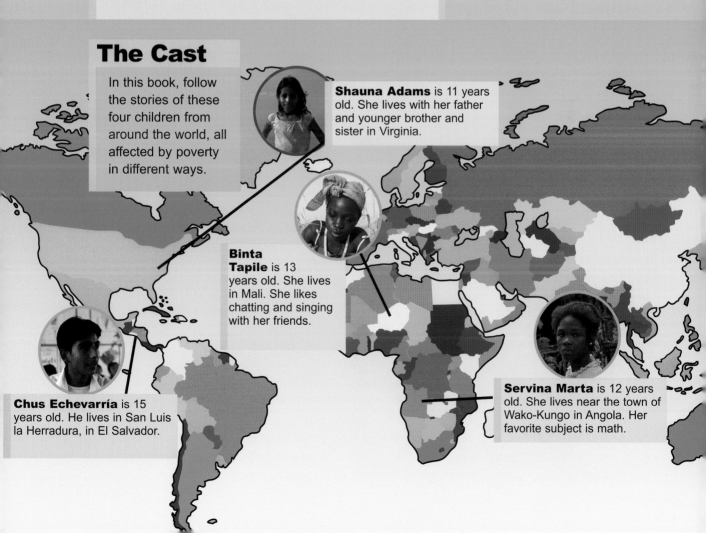

In this book, follow the stories of these four children from around the world, all affected by poverty in different ways.

Shauna Adams is 11 years old. She lives with her father and younger brother and sister in Virginia.

Binta Tapile is 13 years old. She lives in Mali. She likes chatting and singing with her friends.

Chus Echevarría is 15 years old. He lives in San Luis la Herradura, in El Salvador.

Servina Marta is 12 years old. She lives near the town of Wako-Kungo in Angola. Her favorite subject is math.

Living well

We all need food, water, and shelter to survive. Fortunately, many of us don't have to worry about these things. We have water in our faucets, food on our plates, and a home to return to each night.

Food

Food is one of our most basic needs. Eating plenty of different types of food helps us grow strong and stay healthy. It keeps our brains and bodies working and can even prevent some diseases. For most of us, mealtimes are an important part of each day.

 This supermarket offers shoppers a selection of food from all over the world.

ᏝᏝ We get to choose what we want. My favorite is baked potato with cheese. It fills me up for the afternoon. 𐰀𐰀

James, nine years old, lives in Scotland. He likes eating school lunches.

Where does it come from?

We either grow our food ourselves or buy it in stores and markets. In more developed countries, there is a huge variety to choose from. This is partly because developed countries can afford to package or freeze food and transport it long distances. They can also afford to import different foods from other countries around the world.

This Indian family are sharing a nutritious meal together. There is plenty of delicious food to eat.

Too much food?

Many wealthier countries actually produce too much food. Much of this good, nutritious produce is wasted when it passes its sell-by-date—the date after which food experts say it is no longer safe to eat. At the end of the day it is simply thrown away.

> " More than one quarter of America's food, or about 96 billion pounds (43 billion kg) of food a year, goes to waste—in fields, kitchens, manufacturing plants, markets, schools, and restaurants. "

A statistic from the U.S. Environmental Agency. Much of the food we throw away is perfectly safe to eat.

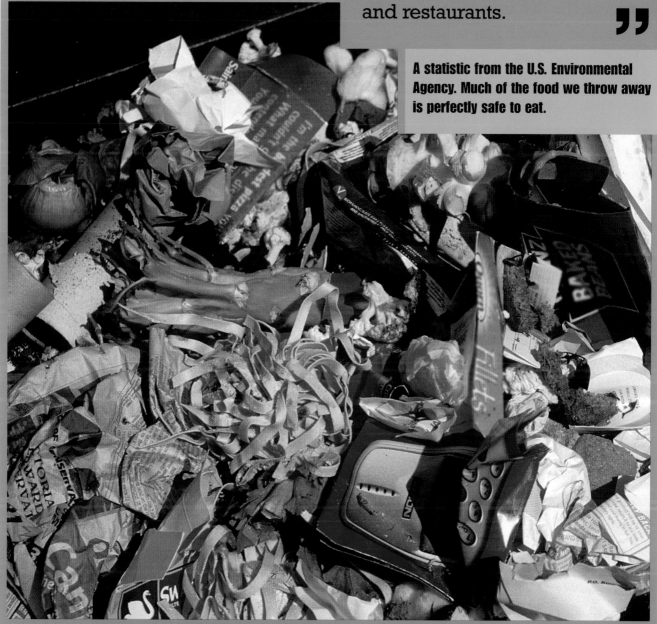

What will you eat and drink today? Where has it come from? How can you find out?

Feeling hungry

What happens when you feel hungry? Do you get tired? Do you find it difficult to concentrate on anything else? We soon feel better if we eat a snack or sit down to a meal. Food is never far away. However, for some people, obtaining food is not so easy.

Binta Tapile from Mali describes how she struggled to find enough to eat last year when crops were destroyed by grasshoppers.

> **"** Sometimes I'd sleep without eating. It's very difficult and I don't like it. You spend the night hungry and in the morning it's worse. **"**

▲ A mother and her children beg for food in Jaipur, India.

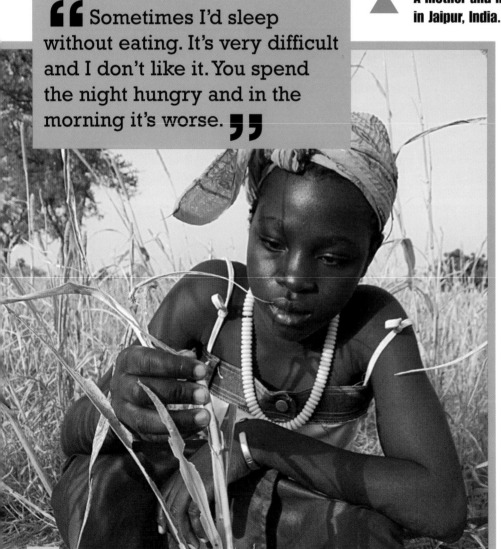

Not enough to eat

In some parts of the world, people are starving. This means that they will die unless they obtain something to eat. In many more parts of the world, people do manage to buy or grow some food but they are still not getting enough food or the right food to keep them healthy. They face a daily struggle to feed themselves and their families. They are malnourished.

The effects of hunger

Food gives us energy. Without it, we feel irritable. Our bodies cannot grow properly and we may feel too weak to study or earn money. We are unable to concentrate. We are also much less able to fight off sickness and disease.

Today, nearly one in seven people worldwide do not get enough food to be healthy and live an active life. This is despite the fact that many people in the developed world have more than enough to eat.

The round bellies of these children are caused by a severe lack of the kinds of food they need for growth and energy.

The effects of starvation are very serious. Binta describes what happened when she went without food for a while.

" We had six days with no food at all. I was very skinny, I was sick, my stomach hurt, and I had pains all over. I couldn't walk. I felt light-headed. "

? **Why is a healthy diet particularly important for children like Binta?**

Under a dollar a day

What can you buy for one dollar or about 50 cents? Potato chips? A carton of juice? It won't stop you from feeling hungry for very long. Yet more than one-fifth of the world's population survive on less than a dollar each day.

The "poverty trap"

The main reason for hunger is poverty. People do not have enough money to get the food they need. And a hungry person is less able to earn money because they have no time or energy to work or learn new skills. All their strength is taken up with trying to secure the next meal for their families. So they remain poor. This is known as the "poverty trap."

Chus Echevarría lives in El Salvador with his brother and sister and her family. He helps support his family.

Chus goes to school in the morning and works collecting crabs in the evening.

" The work we do to earn our food is not easy. I began working when I was eight. I help my sister's husband catch crabs and carry them for him. **"**

❝ I keep a dozen of the crabs we catch to feed the family: that's enough for two meals, lunch and supper (the crabs are very small). **❞**

Chus uses the money he earns to buy bread for his family. His sister Domenica prepares the crabs Chus has caught.

Children in poverty

Many children around the world must work in order to buy or grow food for themselves and their families. But children who are herding cattle, fetching water, or selling vegetables all day cannot go to school to learn the skills they need to escape the poverty trap. Other children must work as well as going to school. School means they have a better chance of leaving the poverty trap, but their day is often long and hard.

Chus earns around a dollar a day from the crabs he catches. Once money has been used to pay for food, Chus spends what is left on school books and his school uniform.

 How is Chus's life different from yours?

The world's poor

Billions of people go hungry every day because they cannot afford to buy food. But why don't they have any money? What makes them poor? Poverty is caused by many different things.

▲ A corn crop withers away in the field because of severe drought in Tanzania, Africa.

Drought and war

Drought, or lack of rain, devastates whole regions of the world each year. No rain means crops cannot grow and animals die. Farmers cannot feed their families and have nothing to sell at the market.

War also affects farmers. Crops and animals are stolen, abandoned, or destroyed. People may be forced to leave their homes and farms. They lose their livelihoods.

Servina Marta, age 12, lives with her parents in Angola. When war came, they had to leave their village home and flee to safety. They lost everything. They returned to the village in great poverty.

❝ My mom and dad built a little cabin before they sent for us. There wasn't much food. ❞

Shauna Adams lives in Virginia. Her father works long hours as a truck driver but he doesn't earn enough to pay the bills.

" I can't remember the last time I bought anything for myself. **"**

Jobs and wages

Another reason for poverty is unemployment, when people cannot find work. This may be because they do not have the right skills, or perhaps there aren't enough jobs to go around. Others cannot work because they are sick or disabled.

Many working people are paid very low wages. They may not have the skills needed to find a better job.

◄ Chinese textile manufacturers at work. These women do not earn enough to provide a good quality of living for their families.

? Is poverty a problem in your country? Can you think of any reasons for this?

Coping with famine

In some parts of the world, whole regions suffer from severe food shortages, known as famine. Famine is a particular problem in areas of Asia and Africa where lack of rain or heavy flooding means crops die and farmers cannot feed their families. It disrupts people's lives and causes them to move around in constant search of money and food.

Binta's village in Mali has suffered because of a plague of grasshoppers.

" We have four fields but we had no harvest at all because there has been no rain and the grasshoppers have eaten all our plants. When I think of grasshoppers, I think of famine. I am afraid I will be hungry again. **"**

Famine in Africa

Drought is a main reason for famine in Africa. However, it is not the only reason. War has forced many people to abandon their homes and farms. Diseases such as malaria and HIV/AIDS mean that farmers may be too sick to work. Farming methods are often not very efficient and governments may fail to store enough grain and seed for use in an emergency.

This map of Africa shows the main areas of famine and malnutrition in recent years.

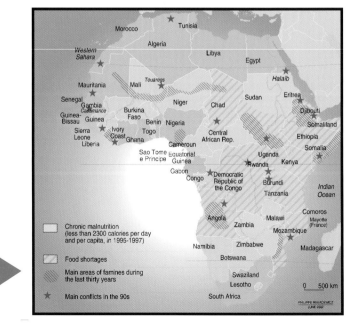

Chronic malnutrition (less than 2300 calories per day and per capita, in 1995-1997)

Food shortages

Main areas of famines during the last thirty years

Main conflicts in the 90s

> " I had to cut firewood and take it to the city to sell. I had to leave home at about 8 o'clock and I got to Wako-Kungo at about 11 o'clock. I carried the firewood on my head. It was very heavy. "

Servina had to travel a long way from her village in order to make money.

Towns and cities

Famine does not just affect farmers. It affects people in towns and cities, too. Food prices go up, which makes it more difficult for people to eat properly. People travel from the countryside to the city to try to find work but often there are not enough jobs to go around. The cycle of poverty continues.

▼ Poor people beg for money in one of the crowded slum areas in Delhi, India. People flock to the city in search of jobs.

? Binta is afraid that she will be hungry again. Do you think the rest of the world should try to help people like her?

The Millennium Development Goals

Poverty is responsible for much of the suffering in the world today. In the year 2000, the world's leaders met at the United Nations and agreed a set of eight goals that would help to make the world a better, fairer place in the 21st century. These goals were named the Millennium Development Goals. The first goal is to get rid of extreme poverty and hunger.

Some of the world leaders who attended the G8 Summit to tackle world poverty.

The Goals

Each goal has particular targets that need to be achieved by the year 2015 and governments have been asked to develop policies that will ensure these targets are met. The target for the first goal is to cut the number of of people living in extreme poverty in half by 2015.

THE EIGHT MILLENNIUM DEVELOPMENT GOALS

1. Get rid of extreme poverty and hunger
2. Primary education for all
3. Promote equal chances for girls and women
4. Reduce child mortality
5. Improve the health of mothers
6. Combat HIV/AIDS, malaria, and other diseases
7. Ensure environmental sustainability
8. Address the special needs of developing countries, including debt and fair trade

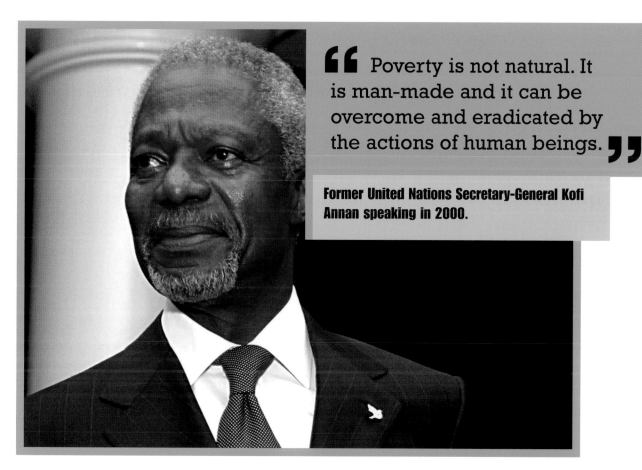

> ❝ Poverty is not natural. It is man-made and it can be overcome and eradicated by the actions of human beings. ❞

Former United Nations Secretary-General Kofi Annan speaking in 2000.

A brighter future

Every child has the right to a life free from poverty and hunger. Binta hopes to become a doctor. Chus wants to be an engineer. The Millennium Development Goals are designed to help them achieve their aims.

Chus hopes to change his life in the future.

> ❝ I'd like to study to be an engineer because I like drawing and they build homes and useful buildings. ❞

? Which Millennium Development Goals would help Binta and Chus make a better life for themselves and those around them?

Emergency aid

Hungry people need food. If they are starving, this food has to be found quickly. There is no time to grow it. It must be brought in from somewhere else. This is known as "emergency aid." Sometimes the government provides it. Sometimes a charity or an aid organization sends it.

Villagers receive emergency aid rations during the war in Iraq.

Access to food

Emergency aid saves millions of lives every year. Once people get food their strength returns and they can begin to farm again, or look for work. Mothers can care for their babies. Children can go back to school. They can start to think about the future.

❝ They gave us 22 pounds of corn and 13 pounds of beans to plant and also some oil, salt, and lentils. If ACM hadn't come to help us, we'd be dead. **❞**

Servina's mother remembers being given emergency aid. Here, Servina's younger sister Rosaria pounds dried corn outside their home.

When people from Servina's village returned to their homes in Angola at the end of the war, crops had been destroyed and they had nothing to eat. An organization called Associaçáo Cristáde Mocidade (ACM) quickly brought in emergency supplies of food for those most at risk of starvation. They gave porridge with added nutrients to the youngest children, and distributed grain to the neediest families. They also gave people corn seeds to plant so that crops could be established again as quickly as possible.

Hunger in the developed world

Hunger and poverty exist in "richer" countries as well as the developing world. Shauna lives in the USA yet her family struggles to make ends meet. They rely on aid from local charities to get by each month.

" Often there isn't enough money to last the month, so we rely on charities such as Save the Children. **"**

Shauna's life is a constant struggle. She has to buy the cheapest food, even though she knows it isn't very healthy.

? Millions of people rely on emergency aid for their survival. Can you think of any problems this might create?

Government action

Emergency aid solves the problem of hunger, but it does not solve the problem of poverty. Poverty can only be ended when people no longer depend on emergency aid. They need to be able to grow their own food and earn their own money. For this to happen, a different kind of help is needed.

What governments can do

Governments can agree to change things so that poor people have the freedom, the knowledge, and the tools to help themselves in the future. They can support poorer farmers, helping them to use the land in a more efficient way. They can change the rules of international trade so that poorer countries can buy and sell goods for a fairer price. This is called "fair trade." They can make sure that resources are shared in times of drought or famine.

‟ It's really very simple. When people are hungry they die. So spare me your politics and tell me what you need and how you're going to get it to these people. ”

▼ The FAIRTRADE Mark shows that the producer has been given a fair price and a better deal.

The singer Bob Geldof (shown above left with Jacques Chirac (center) and Bono) uses the slogan "Make Poverty History" to persuade world leaders to change their policies and reduce the debts of poorer countries.

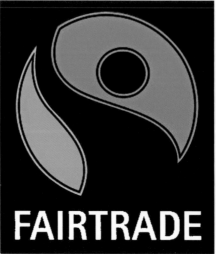

FAIRTRADE

Guarantees a **better deal** for Third World Producers

Debt

One of the biggest problems for poor countries is debt. They borrow money from more developed countries but they can't afford to pay this money back. Now some governments have agreed to reduce the amount of money owed to them. This means that poorer countries have more money to spend on improving the lives of their own people.

▲ A delegation of African women deliver over 150,000 white band cards to Tony Blair from supporters of the "Make Poverty History" campaign, demanding that Britain does more to ensure better aid, fairer trade, and no more debt.

Chus was asked what he would do if he was president for a day.

❝ I'd send help to all those with no resources. ❞

? **What would you do if you were in charge for the day?**

Local solutions

Change at local level is just as important in improving the lives of children like Binta, Servina, Chus, and Jessie. All over the world, charities and community support groups are bringing about lasting change through local solutions to specific problems.

Belco Seiba is a brigadier (see below) from Binta's village, who trains villagers to prevent grasshopper crop destruction.

" The brigadiers have trained the rest of the community to dig for the egg larvae. For one piece of larvae we are securing 85–110 square feet of crops. **"**

A pesticide spray used to protect crops.

A bowl of grasshopper eggs collected by Binta.

New tools and skills

Charities and community support groups give practical help at a local level. This includes providing the right tools and seeds so that people can begin to grow their own food. Teaching people new skills is equally important if they are to farm more efficiently, or find better-paid work.

Helping people help themselves

To fight the grasshoppers in Mali, Binta's village have a team of APH/Christian Aid funded brigadiers (leaders). Volunteers from the community are trained to monitor locust and grasshopper movements, and protect and spray crops.

> **❝**If I get a lot of eggs I take them home for my mother, and as soon as we have collected enough we rush off to exchange them for millet.**❞**

Binta and her friends are destroying grasshopper eggs. She helped collect them.

APH also tried to prevent the insects from coming back by asking people to find and destroy grasshopper eggs. For every two pounds of eggs that were destroyed, APH handed out four pounds of millet in reward.

Long-term benefits

When a charity or a local support group introduces new skills and resources into a community, the benefits often last a long time. Building a water-storage tank, introducing drought-resistant crops, or providing information about good health practices mean that people will be able to take care of themselves and cope better with any problems in the future.

? ▪ APH have given seeds to the women in Binta's village so that they can grow onions. How will this help Binta and her mother?

People who help

Some of the people who work for aid organizations are volunteers. Others are employed because of their skills as nutritionists, agricultural experts, scientists, or managers. All of them want to help improve the lives of those living in poverty.

Different backgrounds

People who work for change come from all sorts of backgrounds, cultures, and faiths. Some come from more developed countries and bring specialized skills. Aid organizations also try to employ local people who have a good understanding of the problems in their particular region.

Teaching skills

William Anderson manages a drought recovery program for Christian Aid in Zimbabwe. He sees it as his duty to pass on the skills that will allow people to help themselves in the future. This kind of action is happening across poor areas in Africa, South America, and areas of the developed world where people are not so fortunate.

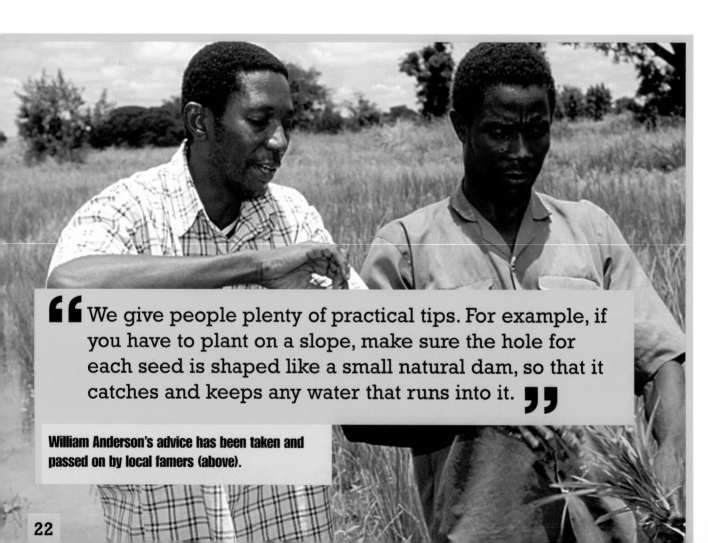

" We give people plenty of practical tips. For example, if you have to plant on a slope, make sure the hole for each seed is shaped like a small natural dam, so that it catches and keeps any water that runs into it. "

William Anderson's advice has been taken and passed on by local famers (above).

Aprodehni in action

Gloria Ventura de Rivera was the director of Aprodehni, an organization that assists people in the area of El Salvador where Chus lives. This is what happened when Hurricane Stan struck the region.

> **ff** Aprodehni goes into action when there's a red alert. We had to distribute food, despite the danger, and children were the priority. **JJ**

When Hurricane Stan struck Chus's village, he worked with Aprodehni to fill sandbags and build up a flood defense system.

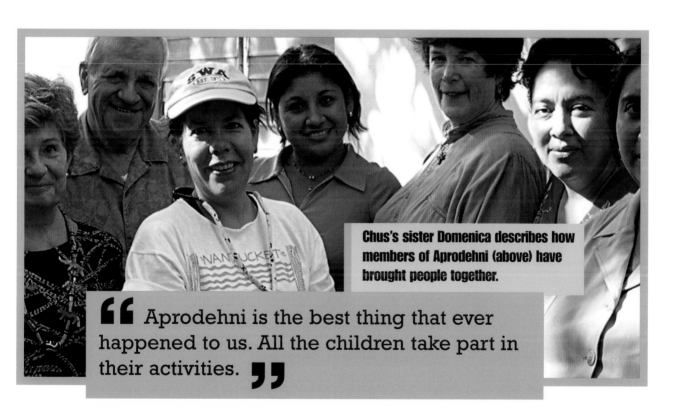

Chus's sister Domenica describes how members of Aprodehni (above) have brought people together.

> **ff** Aprodehni is the best thing that ever happened to us. All the children take part in their activities. **JJ**

? **Have you ever tried to help someone who is having problems? How did it make you feel?**

Growing food

Ending hunger is not just about providing food now. It is about making sure that people can get it in the future. For millions of people around the world, the only way to do this is to grow it themselves.

Teaching people to grow nutritious crops such as rice (right) and wheat is essential to helping them escape from poverty in the long term.

Getting started

When Servina's family returned to their village after the war in Angola, a local organization called ACM came and gave them food to eat. They also gave them the tools and seeds they needed to grow corn and beans. Some of the crops were attacked by insects the first year, and didn't grow well. However, the following year they had enough corn left to plant a bigger crop.

Servina enjoys the family's improved diet.

" We had *funge* (a kind of flour pudding) and beans this morning and we will have funge and pumpkin leaves for lunch. We'll have something for dinner. "

Enough for everyone

Now Servina's family has been given a pair of oxen and a plow. This means that they will be able to cultivate even more land. In the future they hope to be able to grow enough food to sell some of it and return some to ACM so that others can benefit from it. They also hope that ACM will give them some goats, which are good for milk and meat.

❝ We bought 12 oxen to deliver to six families in six different villages. The calves will be given to other families in the village. Other families will also be able to borrow the plow and the oxen. **❞**

Nunes de Oliveira Mario, ACM's project coordinator, explains how the oxen will be used.

❝ I like the oxen. They don't have names yet but I want to call the girl ox Umba. I like Umba best. The other one has horns and I'm a bit scared of him. **❞**

The oxen will help to bring Servina's family out of poverty.

? Now that Servina has more to eat, what difference will this make to her life?

Equal opportunities

Poverty affects children in many ways. It affects the food they eat, the homes they live in, and limits their access to good healthcare, sports, and a proper education. Ultimately a child trapped in poverty does not have the same chances as other children.

❝ I want to get good grades at school, go to school dances, and get into college. **❞**

Shauna states her ambitions for the future.

Shauna's story

Shauna Adams lives in Virginia with her father and younger brother and sister. The family isn't starving and Shauna's father has a job but his wages are low. Shauna, who takes care of the other children before and after school, is forced to buy cheap processed food that is bad for their health. Shauna dreams of going to college but worries that she may have to stay at home to provide for the family and look after her father who has a heart condition and who cannot afford health insurance.

Shauna has few places to go where she lives. She spends a lot of time at the local community center (left).

❝ The problem around here is that they don't teach you how to dream. **❞**

A better life

Some children in Shauna's area are being supported by Upward Bound, an organization that helps poorer children go to college by offering advice on how to improve their grades and get a scholarship so that they do not have to pay expensive tuition fees. Others can join Step-by-Step, a local organization in her area that runs youth programs to build confidence and self-esteem. With the right guidance, children from poorer backgrounds all over the world can be encouraged to raise their expectations and look toward gaining a proper education.

 U.S. organizations such as the state-run Upward Bound program aim to help American children like Shauna realize their dreams.

" Kids need to be given the opportunity to create success. Without money or resources, it's difficult for them to build a bigger world for themselves. "

Michael Tierney, Director of Step-by-Step, explaining why the poorest children need a helping hand to make a start in life.

? Children like Shauna need support from their peers as well as money. How could you help someone like Shauna?

Action you can take

Everyone can take part in the fight against hunger and poverty. One of the most useful things you can do is to make other people aware of the problem. The more people want change, the more change is likely to happen.

Buy fairly traded goods

Look for brands of coffee, sugar, tea, chocolate, fruit, and other goods that carry the Fairtrade symbol. This means that the farmers or producers in developing countries have been paid a fair price for their goods.

Have a "poverty awareness" assembly

Research the reasons for poverty and hunger in a developing country. Use role play to act out a day in the life of a child living in poverty. Then show how, from small beginnings (a few seeds, a goat, a new water pipe) people can start to help themselves and those around them.

Hold a "hunger lunch"

Ask people to go without their usual snacks and offer a bowl of rice or porridge and water instead. The money saved can be collected and donated to a charity helping children in poverty.

▲ Indian sportsman Sachin Tendulkar promotes the UN's "Stand Up Against Poverty" campaign.

▲ Women collect tea in Nepal for sale around the world under the Fairtrade agreement.

christian aid We believe in life before death

The official logo of the charity Christian Aid, which helps poor children around the world, whatever their religion.

Support a charity

There are many charities working around the world to help people escape the "poverty trap." Choose one and ask them for a schools' pack, posters, and information about the work they do. Then start fundraising!

Donating unwanted clothes and other goods is a great way to help people in the developing world.

Donate clothes, shoes, and food

Some charities collect used clothes, shoes, and items such as glasses to be used again in developing countries. Others run local "food banks" where you can donate dried or canned food. Find out what these charities do and then think about setting up a collection point at your school.

? If you could meet Chus, Binta, Servina, or Shauna, what would you like to say to them?

Glossary

Charity an organization that uses money donated by members of the public to help others

Debt money that has been borrowed and must be paid back

Developed world countries with more wealthy economies

Developing world poorer countries with poorer economies

Diet what someone usually eats

Drought prolonged lack of rain

Economy The wealth of a country

Fair trade buying goods at a price that ensures farmers and producers have enough to live on and gives long-term commitments

Famine severe food shortages in a particular area, often because of drought or war

HIV/AIDS a disease that leaves the body unable to fight off illness

Malnourished someone lacking the food necessary for good health and growth

Millennium Development Goals (MDGs) eight goals agreed by world leaders in the year 2000 with the aim of eradicating poverty and promoting the rights of disadvantaged people

Mortality rate the number of deaths in a population

Nutritious healthy food that gives us energy and helps us grow

Poverty lack of money for essential items such as food, shelter, medicines, or education

Resources things that assist development, such as books, equipment, food, seeds, and tools

Starving dying from lack of food

Summit a meeting of world leaders

Sustainability something that is designed for the long term

United Nations an organization of countries around the world with the aim of promoting peace, development, and human rights

Find out more

Useful websites

www.un.org/cyberschoolbus
Scroll down to the Millennium Development Goals for accessible and child-friendly facts about the MDGs. Also useful for information about the work of the United Nations.

www.millenniumcampaign.org/goals_poverty
The latest news, pictures, facts, and statistics as well as information about what you can do to help eradicate hunger and poverty.

www.makepovertyhistory.org
The website of the antipoverty movement.

www.maketradefair.com
Find out about fair trade products, news, and campaigns where you live by clicking on the country links.

www.papapaa.org
An interactive site for children aged 9–14 that focuses on the need for fair trade practices in cocoa farming.

www.care.org
Care says the best way to fight poverty is to invest in girls and there is no better investment than education. They also provide lifesaving assistance to families suffering from major environmental disasters, such as floods.

Note to parents and teachers:
Every effort has been made by the Publishers to ensure that these websites are suitable for children, that they are of the highest educational value, and that they contain no inappropriate or offensive material. However, because of the nature of the Internet, it is impossible to guarantee that the contents of these sites will not be altered. We strongly advise that Internet access be supervised by a responsible adult.

Christian Aid websites

Christian Aid contributed three of the real-life stories in this book (the accounts of Chus, Binta, and Servina). You can find out more about this organization by following the links below:

www.christian-aid.org.uk
The main site for the charity Christian Aid, which helps disadvantaged children and adults all over the world, regardless of their religion.

Index